The Gracie Series

Prais

"The stories are fun to read. They are funny!" ~Aaliyah, 5th Grader

"The stories are engaging and thought-provoking!" ~D. Cain, Grandmother of 9

"The series is perfect for teaching sequencing to emerging and primary readers."
~L. Moots, Elementary Teacher

"The books are engaging, excited to get to the end!" ~C. Bonness, Retired Teacher

"Gracie is a very determined little girl!" ~A. Miller, Elementary School Social Worker

About The Gracie Series

The Gracie Series, written and illustrated by Grace LaJoy Henderson, follows the lovable character Gracie as she gets caught up in funny situations. Parents, teachers and librarians will enjoy sharing these engaging stories and listening as the children share their thoughts sparked by the discussion questions in the back of each book.

The Gracie Series consists of six books: *Popcorn Behind the Bush, Cake in My Shoe, Water in His Face, Math on the Table, I Trimmed My Edges,* and *Puppy Ate My Shorts!* Each story was inspired by entertaining memories from the author's own life, hence the name Gracie; teaching valuable life lessons while inspiring young readers to use reason, analyze and think critically.

Your child will love these heart-warming stories and so will you!

Each book in the series is sold separately at Amazon.com
Available in Kindle eBook, soft cover, and hard cover
Ask for it in book stores and libraries
Published by Inspirations by Grace LaJoy
www.gracelajoy.com

Grace LaJoy
11-23-19

Water in His Face
Copyright 2017. Grace LaJoy Henderson
Written and Illustrated by Grace LaJoy Henderson
Published by Inspirations by Grace LaJoy
Raymore, MO 64083

ISBN: 978-0-9987117-6-8

Printed in the United States of America

The Gracie Series

Water in His Face

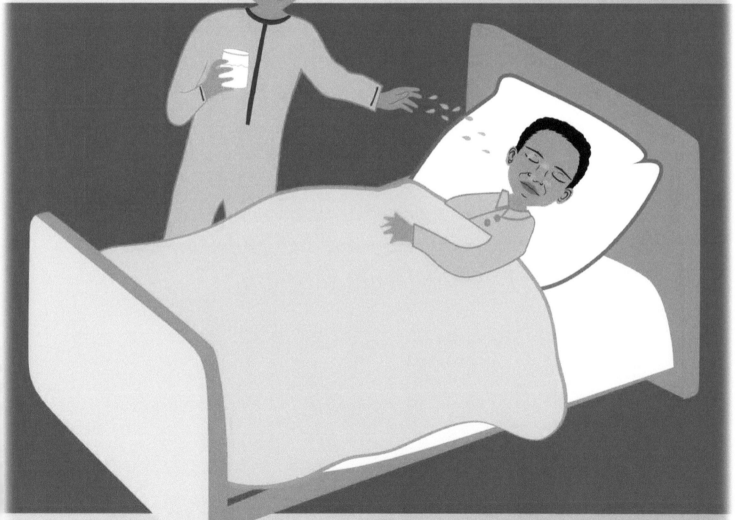

Grace LaJoy Henderson, Ph.D.

It was a school day. Gracie woke up, washed her face, and was preparing to get dressed for school. She was still wearing her pajamas when Mother stormed into her bedroom with a frustrated look on her face.

"Help!" said Mother. "Your brother is supposed to catch the early school bus this morning. I have tried to wake him up three times! But each time, he keeps on sleeping and does not move!"

Understanding how hard it must be for him to wake up earlier than usual, they began to smile. Then Mother asked, "Gracie, will you please go into his room and see if you can get him to wake up, wash up, brush his teeth, put on his clothes and get ready for school?"

"Sure I will!" said Gracie. "I have a great idea!" Gracie eagerly picked up her bull horn. Then she walked with confidence into her brother's bedroom where he was still sleeping soundly. She put the bull horn up to her mouth and shouted, "Wake up!" Brother kept sleeping and did not move.

Gracie felt surprised because her great idea did not work.

"I have another idea!" thought Gracie. She ran towards her brother's bed as fast as she could, leaped on top of the mattress, and began to jump up and down as hard as she could! But again, Brother kept sleeping and did not move.

Gracie felt disappointed because her second idea did not work.

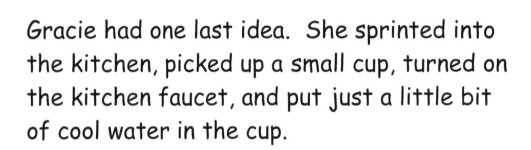

Gracie had one last idea. She sprinted into the kitchen, picked up a small cup, turned on the kitchen faucet, and put just a little bit of cool water in the cup.

Excited about her idea, she rushed back into
her brother's room and stood beside his bed.
She dipped the tips of her fingers into the
cup and shouted, "It's raining!" Then she
playfully flicked water from her fingers into
her brother's face.

Up jumped Brother thinking it was raining! Instantly, he realized it was not raining, but he could not fall back to sleep. He was now wide awake.

Gracie walked away feeling proud of herself
because she finally came up with an idea that
caused her brother to wake up! As she left
the room, Brother lay there with his eyes
wide open and water on his face.

Noticing the time, Brother realized he could be late for the early school bus, so he leaped out of bed and stretched.

Then he ran into the bathroom, washed up,
brushed his teeth and began putting on his
school clothes.

When Mother saw him out of bed and ready
for school, she was shocked!

"How did you get your brother to wake up?"
asked Mother.

Gracie replied with a big smile, "Oh, just a
little water in his face."

The End

What do you think?

1. When Gracie's "bull horn" idea didn't work, what did she do next to try to wake up her brother?
2. Pretend you were Gracie. Now, name some things you would have done to wake up Brother.
3. Have you ever tried to do something, but, it didn't work the first time? If so, what did you do next?

The Gracie Series

Collect them all!

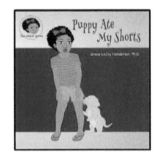

About the Author

Grace LaJoy Henderson has earned a PhD in Christian Counseling with an emphasis in Writing and Research. Her graduate degrees are in the fields of Education, and Curriculum and Instruction. Her undergraduate degree is in Social Psychology. She has served youth in public school, church and community settings. She enjoys talking, reading stories and sharing poetry with youth and adult groups.

CPSIA information can be obtained
at www.ICGtesting.com
Printed in the USA
BVHW02n1501220618
519692BV00002B/23/P

*9 7 8 0 9 9 8 7 1 1 7 6 8 *